HONOUR

BIN SOBCHUK

HONOUR

This is a work of fiction. All of the characters, names, incidents, organizations, and dialogue in this novel are either the products of the author's imagination or are used fictitiously.

iUniverse books may be ordered through booksellers or by contacting:

iUniverse
1663 Liberty Drive
Bloomington, IN 47403
www.iuniverse.com
844-349-9409

ISBN: 978-1-6632-3894-8 (sc)
ISBN: 978-1-6632-3893-1 (e)

Library of Congress Control Number: 2022910354

Print information available on the last page.

iUniverse rev. date: 06/23/2022

Contents

Honours

Maxwell is a police officer. How did he become a policeman? Young Max was active and did not have many big goals. He liked friendship and some sports. He also spoke up for the oppressed. He studied yet did not do very well. Once he got a B-, he was very humiliated. He went home to read the white test paper. He kneaded it into a ball and dropped into garbage bucket. "Kneel down." His father commanded. He was embarrassed and kneeled down in front of his father. His father picked up the paper ball and opened to see it. He said, "Son the marks symbolize honours" Max nodded his head. He studied hard since then, yet he knew that his goals were higher than that. When he was seventeen, he accomplished his high school and went to Police Academy as a cadet. He was excellent. He completed Police Academy and became a police officer. When he first wore the police uniform at home, his parents were overjoyed and cried. His father told him, "Although we are old, we do not need your money. Take care, my only child." He was still naughty and laughed to say "One heart two ways." His father did not smile and said to him- Honours.

He likes fight training. He is very good at it. He likes guns and the power that is why he choose not to be a police dog trainer. He knew that if he had a dog, he had a faithful friend. His beginning jobs were not very exciting. He was promoted from constable level one to level three. He saw some peels getting protection money or dealing with under the table money. He has not done any of these. In his mind, he wants a sunshine salary. He also sees that some old police officers remain as police constables for their whole lives. He believes that they are not like him at all. He volunteers his services to seize drugs or drug dealers.

He knew that it means money and power. Yet it is dangerous too. His first-hand experience makes him very confident. He does not want his parents and himself to be disappointed. During the first time anti-drug operation, he saw a lot of cash he and did not believe that he is on the spot and not in front of the TV. He gunned down the second leader of the ring and fought to rescue his colleague. He gets the first rank medal and is promoted to sergeant. One thing is that his salary does not go up, because in police stations, promotions and raising salaries usually are not at the same pace. He loves guns which makes him less afraid. Drug dealers are very dangerous. If you are caught, they just use their drugs on you; you will have no future. Some police officers are struggling from addiction and live in pain mentally and physically. He knew that for drug dealers guns are his first choice. He did not fear gunfire. He experienced drug factory's armed forces. In a fierce exchange of gunfire, he gunned down many of them and survived. Finally the police task force occupied the factory and got tons of drugs. He gets a second promotion to staff sergeant. Now his salary is over 100, 000 dollars. He gets a sunshine salary. He writes letters to his parents and uses "Honours" as the title and takes photos with his staff sergeant uniform. He is 30 years old now. His parents are proud of him. He announces that his money is clean.

Maxwell is married and has kids. His parents often help them by taking care of the kids and enjoy their companionship. They and Max teach all the children to be good and cherish their honours. The kids see Maxwell's uniform and cheer "Daddy we want to be a police officer just like you!"

Buddy and His Vet

Buddy is a one year old German Sheppard dog. He is handsome and clever. He likes his vet and can talk to him too. Today, Buddy has diarrhea. I take him to his vet. Buddy saw the vet and whimpered. His vet let me wait outside and they talk together. Buddy is sad and complains, "Vet, my mom did not buy me clothes. I saw that other dogs have beautiful clothes; I also want some." The vet said to him, "You have a shiny fur coat, you do not need clothes at all. Also German Sheppard dogs can handle cold weather." Buddy is very upset and barks to the vet "Measure my chest, waist and hip; I want you to make clothes to me." The vet smiles and said, "I did not measure your mom's three measurements. I seldom see her wearing new clothes." Buddy cries and woofs, "Do not mention her. She has no three measurements. She is over 270 pounds." The vet becomes serious and talks to Buddy, "Your mom feeds you very good food. You enjoy love and care. Today you have diarrhea, just because you over eat. Not many owners could send their pets to vets all the time." Buddy stop crying and nods his head. "I love my mom and please do not tell her what I said." The vet lets me come in. he said to me, "Today, I do not charge you money. Go home and do not feed Buddy for one day. If he still has diarrhea, come back and see me."

Time flies, but Buddy never forgets what his vet said to him.

Buddy Goes To a New Home

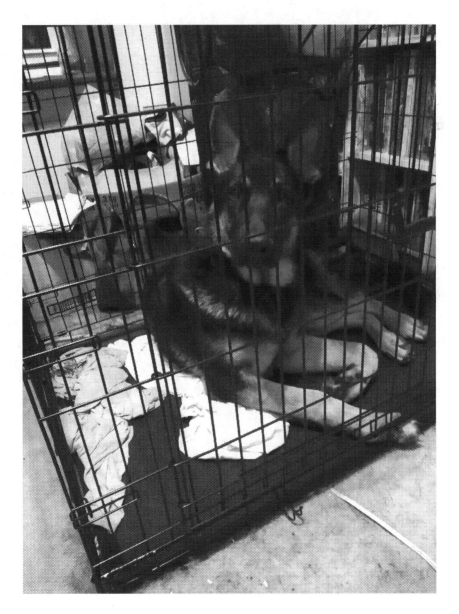

I have arthritis in my knees. I cannot walk Buddy. I need to pay dog walkers for walking Buddy. I love him, yet I know that it is time to find a new home for Buddy. I still remember that the first day Buddy went to my home. My friend told me that I should accompany him the first night, because he might miss his parents and brothers. (His parents gave birth to six boys and no girls.) I put him on the first floor, since he was so young at eight weeks, that he could not climb the stairs. At 2 AM, he was tired like me. I had him sleep on the floor since my house has no bed rooms on the first floor. I felt very happy and unforgettable. I have never been pregnant but I have a cat and a puppy who are my fur ball sons.

Buddy does not like cats. My cat (Prince) was scared by his barking and hides in the basement for almost two months. Then I placed Prince on the second floor. They were all at peace. Now Buddy grew up and often ran up and down the stairs. My cat felt nervous. He always hides under the quilt even on the sunny days. Once Buddy chased Prince and broke the vase. Prince was hurt and his nails were broken and bleeding. I gave Prince to my church friend. I cried many times. I love Buddy. He is my first dog in my entire life. I promised that he would be also my last dog. He is my special baby. Buddy is playful. He always was getting into mischief. He ripped all my twelve pillows and many of my quilts. He chewed up my two new pairs of eyeglasses, which cost 750 dollars. He ripped my books which are my late husband's fortune. He destroyed my clothes. I am over weight so my clothes are much more expensive than regular ones. He sometimes bit me. My arms and body had many bruises. His medicines and exams expense cannot be counted. I spent 2500 dollars sending him to a doggy training school. Besides the tuition, the food and treats cost over 200 dollars. He was neutered which cost 600 dollars. My neighbour is the owner of Pet Value who helped me order a very big dog crate for 300 dollars. That is Buddy's favorite crate. The first one was a little bit smaller when he was one year old.

Today, my neighbour who loves Buddy has a friend who wants Buddy. They came to my home. I put halter head collar and leash for Buddy. I also gave them many dog food cans, two big bags of dry dog food, his medicine, mouth wash, muzzle, toys, training pat, and treats etc. I asked the new owner what was the new name for Buddy? He said that he would keep his name Buddy. I was very appreciative. I told him that Buddy loves his big crate. He said that after couple of days, they will come and get it for Buddy. I watch Buddy get into the car and they drove away. I went home. I saw the empty crate on the first floor. I cried loudly. I could not forget that I applied for his licence on March 11th, 2010. That day I went to hospital for my contraception surgery. On the one hand, I felt Buddy is my last dog, (he is also my first dog.) on the other hand, I felt scared to make love especially to become pregnant. I did not have sex for years, because I am a widow.

At night, I looked at my cell phone. The new owner sent me his farm's pictures. He has sheep, seven horses, four dogs, three cats and his house. I called his new owner John who told me that Buddy likes his new home and Buddy heard my voice and smiled. I was relaxed and wished that Buddy had a new good home.

Miss Buddy

Today, I saw two German Sheppard dogs near my home. I cried. I miss my Buddy. One German Sheppard dog is exactly like Buddy. Two teenage girls walked him. I am not good at walking dogs. Buddy is big and strong. He is also independent. He likes running by himself. Some neighbours are not kind. They sent emails to all of the neighbours with my name, my dog's breed and name and my home address. They wanted the pictures to send to the police in charge of animals so they would fine me. I felt very sad and gave Buddy to a farm owner. I am depressed and always weep. One of my neighbours saw me shed tears. She gave me five tulips to cheer me up. I am very appreciative.

I love my dog. He is my son. I always forgive him for his mistakes. He also brings me happiness and company. When Buddy just went to my home, he was eight weeks old and twenty pounds. Now he is one year four months old, and ninety pounds. All my neighbours and friends said that Buddy is beautiful. I always said that he is handsome. Buddy has two police friends. They sometimes go to my home to see him and even walk him. Many people think that Buddy is a police dog. Buddy saved my life once. December 2020, I was sick with mental illness. I did not sleep for days. Once I was awake after 1am, suddenly, someone knocked my door very loud. I instinct wanted to open my door; Buddy immediately loudly barked. I was scared by the knocking sound. I thought that it was ghost doing the knocking. I did not open the door. Now every time I think about this thing, I thank Buddy very much.

Recently, I often dream that Buddy ran back to my house or got lost on the way home. I cannot drive. I wish that I could take the long distance bus to see him, yet the new owner John said that his house is still far from the bus stop. John sent me some video from his phone. I saw Buddy eating dog food and looking happy. I also feel happy. Buddy sometimes is naughty but still unforgettable.

Internet Fraud

People often talk about internet fraud. I was lucky to avoid some. Two weeks ago,
I found some emails from a person named Rick Collins. He said that he is
an army officer. His rank is Master Sergeant. He wants to make friends with
me. Since COVID-19, people are all stuck at home, with no social activities and
parties. I could not find a boyfriend and was very frustrated. I emailed him back.
Then we had an online chat.

He sent me some photos. In the meantime, he let me send some pictures to
him. From these pictures, I saw that he is a white man, with blue eyes, and about
6 feet height. Some pictures shows that he wears uniforms with long guns. I told
him that I am in Canada, I do not want to live in USA. He said that he could live
with me in Canada. Then we began to chat. He always sends me kissing symbols
and says he loves me. I began to falling in love with him and opened my heart to
him. I also ask him some questions, for example: do you smoke or drink? How
old are you? etc. His answers are sometimes inconsistent. Yet, he could find some
reasons to cover it up. I did not think too much. He said that he is divorced with
one daughter.

His daughter is in her twenties and lives with her mom in South Africa. He also
said that in camps, soldiers cannot make a phone call or even go on the internet.
He needs to go to the internet under the table. He called me once, but he said
that I cannot call him. I felt that his English has an Arabic accent. He said that he
worked in Iraq, and Syria. We have a seven hours' time difference. I doubted his
sincerity, but his romantic love words and symbols cover this up again. We talked
about our childhoods, our different philosophies, and our bright future. He said

that for me, he would do anything to live with me. I said that you are a soldier and mechanical engineer; it is easy to find a professional job in Canada. I was moved. We talked about how to immigrant to Canada. Finally we decided to marry and I would sponsor him to Canada. I even called the Immigrant companies to do so, but they said that due to COVID-19, USA and Canada border is closed, so they cannot deal with this case right now. He said that he will retire in May 2021. Then he will come to Toronto to deal with it. I was so excited that I could not wait for my darling to show up. Everything seemed fine.

On April 20th, 2021 he told me that it is his daughter's birthday. I said that:

"You give her an extra 200 dollars, and say that I gave it to her. When we meet, I give 200 dollars to you." He wrote that "I cannot send money from here. Very bad. My daughter wanted an iPhone and laptop but I cannot send them to her. Can you send her 2,500 dollars to buy an iPhone and a laptop? I will give it back to you when I come to Toronto. I want to make my daughter happy. I say: "No, we finished." He immediately called me. I did not answered. He wrote that you just stop talking to me just because I ask for a favour? I did not answer and I did not want to. He called me many times and sent me many messages. He wrote that it really hurt, when you do not talk to me…

I felt been cheated. I was depressed for three days. I cannot trust online dating anymore. I should be vigilant all the time.

Love Letters

Jennifer is a writer or say amateur writer. She published one book when she was young. One publisher signed a contract with her to publish two children's books within four years. She was very excited and treated her friends and relatives. They took a photo with her jumping in the air. In 2018, our street had a party. I saw an invitation for studying love letters in the library near my home. I felt curious, so I kept the invitation. Soon the class began. That was the first time I noticed Jennifer. She was our teacher. She bought notebooks and ballpoint pens for us. She taught us how to do creative writing. She helped us to write love letters. I could keep up with what she taught. I like writing so I often read my writing in the class. After three weeks, I told her that I published one book and I hoped that she could read it and gave me some suggestions. I gave her my debut book. In the next class, I brought a big box of fine European chocolate to her. Yet, she did not read my book much, and she said that in my book, the Heroines' fates are very miserable. I thought that she will say I mimic Hemingway's or Shakespeare's works. But, she did not. She saw the chocolate and asked me if I wanted to take it back. I said, no. After 8 weeks, our class was finished. I joked with the teacher, "Jennifer, in North America when a class is finished, usually the teacher will treat the students. Do you want to treat us?" She was immediately upset. I was scared and said that, "I am sorry teacher, please forget it." The last class, she baked the chocolate cupcakes for us. Everybody had one. There was one cupcake left, one of my classmates said that the teacher should give it to me, yet she refused and put it in her bag. Now I recalled her lessons. She taught us many kinds of writing skills, which are very useful. For example, she let us choose different things such as gloves, scarf, pen, toys etc. Then we wrote an essay about what we choose. After that we chose another one and rewrote the essay with a new subject involved. That made the creative writing much easier. She also taught us now to write poetry. Of course she asked everybody to write many love letters about our communities and our people.

In my mind, love letters are emotional, and are artistic conception. Unfortunately, she did not mention religion. In my mind, love letters are real in my heart, which is a smooth overflow. It is not manmade. I remembered that she told us, when her family wanted a house, she was afraid that the owner would not sell it to her family. She wrote love letters to express how they loved and cherished the house. In the end, the owner sold the house to her. One day, I passed her house, I chatted with her neighbour about this story. Her neighbour looked a little bit sad. She told me that she was a good friend with the former owners. They could sell the house for 4000 dollars more, yet Jennifer wrote love letters to show how they loved and cherished her house. She provided details such as the unique decorated veranda, in door glazed tiles, even the old buffet… Finally, they sold the house at a low price. Once the former owners passed the house, they found that their veranda with bikes and children's toys. Their buffet had disappeared. They knew that they had been cheated.

I like to sit down on my veranda and watch people. One day, Jennifer and her two sons passed my house. They yelled that, "Punch and punch back; punch and punch back!" I felt astonished. That is not what Jesus Christ taught us. That is wild, brutal and vicious. How can she teach her sons this concept and also teach adult love letters? She even said that sometimes, the University of Toronto invited her to coach students' lover letters. Further, I have a German Sheppard puppy. He occasional is out of my control. Jennifer and her husband shot the pictures and sent them to the city. City fined me 365 dollars. They even sent emails to my neighbours with my name, my dog's name, breed and my house number. They said that my dog is dangerous. Anyone who sees my dog run away, shoots the photos and sends to the city. The couple used many strong words to frame my puppy. I am scared that city will fine me again. Also I think that my neighbours should be friends. I went to her home to apologize and gave her a big box fine European chocolate. Her husband got the chocolate, and did not say a word and closed the door. I felt strange. At least, I deserve a "thank you". Finally, I gave my puppy to a farm owner. I am very sad. Today, I saw her husband riding a bike with his two sons. He said, "Good Morning." I said "Good Morning." with a smile. It is hard for me for just losing my puppy. Yet, his older son saw me and rolled his eyes at me. I really did not know why I am wrong? I gave them chocolate; I said I was sorry. They made me lose my fur ball son. The city fined me just because they twice shot photos and sent to the city. I am the victim. I learned that love letters are really not from their hearts. They are alien.

I love my church. I love my neighbours. At Easter Monday, 2021 I pray that my puppy and my friends and I will have a warm heart day.

Dennis Tidbits

Dennis was my late husband. He worked as a security officer for 25 years, although he did not like it. He was a very good security guard. He helped others a lot. He had worked in a French school as nighttime security for 3 years. In the morning, a black woman security guard replaced him. That woman security guard never came on time. Every day, Dennis needed to stay one or two hours extra. He never told the manager about that. He even did not let the woman security guard treat him to one cup of coffee.

Dennis mainly worked in the Nestle Chocolate Factory as a nighttime guard. He was integrity and honesty. Nighttime guards' actions were more flexible than daytime guards'. Some young guards did not do routine patrols; instead watched porn videos. Some even had intimate contact. Dennis was very upset, because these should be zero tolerance. Also if factory leaders knew it, the whole security department would be fired. Every time Dennis mentioned it; he would say that because he was cautious and conscientious, he was the longest serving security guard in the Nestle Chocolate Factory. Sometimes the factory was short of guards. Dennis needed to do the job of two people. He spent two hours patrolling the east side of the building and one hour staying at the reception desk to answer the phone. He then spent two hours patrolling the west side building and came back to answer the phone. The whole night was just like this. He felt this was unfair. But to make a living, he had few choices.

Dennis liked Christmas. The factory gave everybody gifts. However, he seldom celebrated Christmas with his parents. He needed to work. Occasionally, the factory gave him Christmas off; he would work for other security companies to earn extra money. If he was lucky, he could get a bottle of liquor. He did not drink. Yet his father liked drinking, so he gave his father a bottle of liquor as a gift for the holidays.

When Dennis was young, his family was not rich. His neighbour' son had a very good silk shirt. When the son grew bigger, the neighbour gave this shirt to Dennis. His mom was very happy. Dennis wear it for many years. His neighbour was called Jim Hunter. That boy was his best friend. He was eight years older than Dennis. He often protected Dennis. Sometimes, he also beat Dennis just like a big brother. In the meantime, if someone bullied Dennis, he always fought back. Once, the worst boy, who wanted to beat his classmates, ran and tried to catch them. Dennis could not run fast and fell down on the ground. Jim Hunter tried his best to let him stand, but he could not. He was just like a bag of 150 pounds potatoes, too heavy. Finally, the bad boy kicked Dennis. When he went home, his mom saw his one black eye.

Dennis' uncle was a famous judge in Hamilton. His mom wanted him to become a corporate lawyer. She bought him many books and read them to him before he fell asleep. His father always said that his mother spoiled him. His mother's efforts had good results. Dennis' English was very good. He often corrected other students' mistakes. Many students thought that he was a genius. In high school, his English teacher said that he was the university material. He did not go to university, instead of he went to Humber College. His majors were Social Work and Library Studies. His first formal job was as a Toronto Star copy boy.

I love Dennis. I wrote this to share his experiences and my loss.

Mirror, Mirror

Prinz is a TTC (Toronto Transit Commission) driver. He has brown hair and blue eyes. His blue eyes are from his mom and he is hairy and over 6 feet tall like his dad. His mother is a German blonde; his father is a black Jamaican. Prinz is a given name from his mother. He likes this German name.

He is a lad and joined TTC over one year ago. He is smart and can handle his job well. Yet, people knew him all call him dark Prinz. He likes his job and also loves women. He is good at using mirrors at the front of buses. There are two mirrors in the front of each bus. One is big; one is small. He often adjusts the small mirror to watch the passengers. He separates the passengers into three groups. One is for those he likes; the other is for who like him. He finds that women he likes, sit down in front and are more active. Women who like him are more passive and sit down a little bit farther away from him. If the ladies like him and he also likes them, he will greeting them first.

Today, he works the morning shift. 71 bus Runnymede route starts at 5:10 am. He watches one lady he likes sitting down beside the driver seat. He stands up and moves the small mirror so he can see her all the time. Drive and enjoy watching the beauties are his favorite hobbies. Prinz is handsome. Many women feel that he is unforgettable at the first sight. Prinz is naughty. He uses his left hand more to control the steering wheel, so he can show the lady that he has no wedding ring in his left hand and his sexy hairy arms. He looks at the road and the mirror. He is disappointed. He finds the lady pays no attention to him. He looks at her left hand, and she is married. Soon a girl who likes him gets on the bus. She is shy, yet today she sits down beside the first girl, because she is jealous of her. Prinz adjusts the mirror, so he can watch both of them at the same time. The second girl is younger and single. She wears safety boots. She is a labourer. Most people who take the bus before 6 am work in factories. Prinz does not like her at all. He drives the bus very fast and shaky. That girl almost vomits on the bus just like a pregnant woman. He knows that she sometimes skips breakfast. Another woman gets on the bus, she always sits down at the end and on the left side of the bus. This time Prinz does not adjust the mirror, because he cannot see her at all. He knows how to let the women fall in love with him. He drives the bus smooth and at even speed, which make the passengers feel refreshed, and heart-to-heart. There are only two people on the bus now. The woman skips her stop and let him drive her to the bus terminal. She feels never better. At the end, she holds her cell phone to talk to Prinz, and wants his phone number. Prinz refuses her offer.

Prinz continues his work. A blonde gets on the bus. He immediately notices her. She sits down in front of the backdoor. He adjusts the mirror, and looks closely. She is a blonde; her hair is tied up. She also notices him, but she pretends not to see him. The bus goes on. He loves her at first sight. He makes eye contact with her many times. Suddenly, she unties her hair; the fair hair is just like a golden waterfall flowing down her lower back. He stunned. It is a red signal. He does not focus and bumps into a car. Prinz is angry. She gets off the bus.

The supervisor comes. He lets Prinz go home first. Prinz comes home. His mom saw him upset. She pats his hair to console him. He grabs his mother's beautiful fair hair and hits her head against the wall. He swears: "Why you did not marry a German?" his mother's navy blue eyes reflect confusion and fear. Prinz watches the wall on the mirror. He dyes his hair to a fair color. He wanders the streets.

Fatty

I knew Fatty recently. Why did I call her Fatty? Because she is over 340 pounds. She is sixty seven years old. Fatty was born into a very big family. Her mom is French; her dad is an indigenous. Her dad married many times and had fifteen children. Fatty is the oldest one. When she was five years old, her mom divorced and sent her to an orphanage. There, Fatty had a miserable life. At that time, Fatty was thin. No one taught her schooling, or even talked to her. She had government child support payments every month, but the orphanage got it and never gave her good food. When she was twelve years old, every morning, a truck came and drove them to farms to work. She had little food every day, so she often felt hungry. Sometimes, she was starving. She ate the food that she just harvested from the earth such as carrots, leeks etc. Once she was really hungry; she ate a raw potato! Now she knew that raw potatoes are dangerous to eat.

Fatty could not tolerate this life. When she was sixteen year old, she fled from the orphanage. The orphanage was near Calgary. She walked beside the highway. A big van stopped in front of her. The driver asked her if she wanted a ride. She said that she wanted to go to a big city. The driver said that they would go to Toronto. She got in the van. Then the nightmare began for this sixteen years old girl. The four men in the truck Gang raped her for four days none-stop. Fatty was very frightened, in pain, sad and even thought of committing suicide. Finally, she was thrown out on the sidewalk in the City of Toronto. She had nowhere to go, but she soon found a job in a restaurant as kitchen help. The restaurant provided her with boarding. She felt that for the first time in her life she ate full and delicious food. After a few months, Fatty always felt tired, her belly was painful, and she vomited. She went to the hospital. The doctor told her that she was pregnant. The doctor asked her who the father was. She told the doctor that she did not know since she was Gang raped in the van. The doctor recommitted the specialist who did an abortion to her.

Fatty married a man five years older than her when she was in her twenties. At that time, she was 180 pounds. Her husband was a junkie. They had a son. The man did not give Fatty much happiness. She needed to take care of her son and work in the factory. When her son was ten years old, she divorced that man. Then she found another man and married. The second husband did not like her son. She gave her son to an orphanage. Her son never connected with her. Soon, she had a daughter. She thought that her second husband could be relied upon. Yet he was an alcoholic and seldom brought money home for her and their daughter. She did not leave him. They married for over 20 years. Finally, her second husband died from cancer.

Her daughter married and had a son, but they divorced. She did not take her son, and married again. She had a son with her second husband. Then she divorced again. She left her second son with his dad. Finally, she married her third husband, and had a son. Her two ex-husbands all married again. Yet, her two sons lived a painful life. They tried to find their mother. She did not want them to see her. The oldest son also became a junkie. Once he called his grandma (Fatty). He said that he missed his mother. Fatty let him come to her home, however she said that he should pay his own transportation fee, and bring some food. Her grandson came. She was not warm-hearted. Just after one day, she let him go. The two grandsons never saw her again.

Fatty likes men. She always wants to find a man and make love with him. She went on-line to find a Zumba coach. She hired him for home visiting teaching at $25 per hour. The coach finished one hour of teaching. She gave him good food. She told him that she wanted to make body contact with him, but he refused. He was not good either. He often sells to Fatty some very expensive nourishment. She just has a limited retirement pension. She could not afford it. The coach said that if she did not buy it, he would stop the training. Once Fatty wanted him to live in her home for three days. The coach agreed. Yet he said that he needed thirty oranges. Every day he would eat ten oranges. She bought thirty oranges. When the coach came and stayed in her home three days, he just wanted to spend Fatty's money and refused to make love with her. Fatty felt very upset and stopped to purchase his nourishment. He did not come to her home anymore. He called her and said that she was too fat, he did not want to marry her.

Fatty likes on-line dating. She fell in love with a man and chatted with him days and nights. She told him her personal information and even her pay day. The man often asked money before her pension came. She did e-transfer 500 USD every month. The handling fee is over 30 CAD. Finally, the man told Fatty that he would go to Toronto. Fatty went to spa for manicure and pedicure. Then she took a taxi to Toronto Person Airport to meet him. Yet the man sent a message: "My passport has expired. I cannot meet you now." She went home alone and with no money left.

Fatty often relies on the food bank. Every month, she needs to pay 500 dollars rent. That leaves 900 dollars for everything else. She does not know how to manage money, so she goes to the two food banks near her home. She also has a big appetite. She can eat five or six apples a day. She has diabetes. At night, she sometimes can eat all the food in her refrigerator.

Fatty is my friend. I do not try to judge her. I just hope that she is safe and happy every day.

Church

I joined the Church of Jesus Christ of Latter-day Saints when I was 29 years old. There I grew up and found meaning for my life. When I was young, I suffered abuse and neglect from my parents. They seldom taught me how to deal with people, and what I should do. Their teaching method was very simple-punishment. I could not tolerate it anymore and I went to Canada from China. The missionaries brought me to the Mormon Church. I went to the Church from casually, to regular, and often. Here I found love and I began to know how happy it is to love and be loved by people. The most important thing is that I know what I should do. I self- studied and was taught by church members what is right and wrong. I followed what I was taught and became normal. I am surrounded by the love of church members, which I never experienced in any other place.

I remembered when I just joined the church, I often made mistakes and was wild. Once in Chinese Lunar New Year, my bishop saw me and said hi to me. I said hi to him. I did not feel anything wrong. In the sacrificed meeting, the bishop used Chinese and said to us "xinnian kuaile" (happy new year). He watched me and spoke twice. I knew that I was wrong. When I just joined the church, I seldom greeted the leaders, because I was shy and I thought nobody knew me. I was so insignificant. The bishop's father who was also a bishop, once greeted me. I knew that I was not invisible. I began to greet them. I knew that the bishop did not like me for a long time, because I made a lot of mistakes. I also had mental illness so that he thought it best to leave me alone. Once I made a big mistake. I had adultery. My bishop and three church leaders interviewed me. After that, the bishop said that I should go to the corridor door to wait the result. When he let me come into the room again, all the four leaders stood up. I immediately said to them that I was not worth having them stand up. Yet the bishop said that I am the God's daughter; I deserved it. I never forget those words. I was being respected even when I was wrong. My parents just knew how to discipline me and seldom respected me if at all. Now I know as a human being what I should do. I should not make the same mistake anymore.

In church, I also had many friends. That is why I love the church. Most of them make me happy. In society, some people are really bad and always cheat you. In church, we love each other and help each other. I love the church's activities. We play together and eat together. Church's banquets are my favorite. Everybody brought some food and we ate together. Since we are from different countries and places, we bring different foods. I open my eyes and enjoy food that I never had before.

Our church members believe eternal marriage. We marry at City Hall and seal the marriage in heaven. Our church has single adult parties and dating. If you want to be a bishop, you must marry first. Many of our church leaders married and have several kids. They are good examples for us. I never forgot that missionaries who went to our home and persuaded my boyfriend to marry me. After we married, we just understood how sweet it is to be a couple rather than a partners. I appreciate our church's teachings.

Our church teaches me and guides me in my life. I should not forget God's words and follow His lead. I hope that I will be more Christian like.

Summer Prince

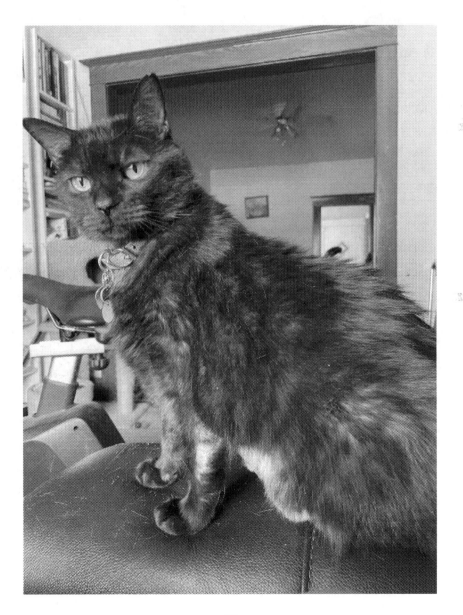

Summer is coming now. Prince (my cat) is eager to find new girlfriends. He often runs away from our house, which makes me worry about him very much. Prince is pampered a lot. He is fed Blue Buffalo Wild brand cat food. He also loves canned food. At the end of September, he will be nine years old, but in my mind, he is still a baby. He is very healthy and active. Because of hot weather, he got a lion cut fur style. He likes it. Prince is a pure black cat. He loves sunshine. He can sleep the whole day in the sunshine. I never blame him for this, since I am lazy too.

Prince is very brave. He often fights with other cats and chases squirrels away from our property. Yet, sometimes he is timid. He is afraid of dogs. My neighbour has two tom cats, one called Johnny, the other called Chandler. Prince fights with them. Prince likes to climb trees. Yet getting down from the trees is a big challenge for him. Prince also loves to catch birds. Once I saw him clawing a Blue Jay, whose dead body was on my lawn the next day. Prince likes to sit on my porch watching the street. He watches cars and pedestrians. Sometimes people look at him and say what a beautiful cat. I feel very glad. Once I went to a library.

I borrowed a DVD to learn cat massage. It is not difficult to recite. From then on, I often massage Prince.

Every week I watch kids learning to speak French. I always let Prince watch with me. Sometimes he likes it and listens; sometimes he just plays near me. He slept yesterday. I was angry and threw him on the floor. He was scared and said moi. I was so happy that Prince can say a French word. My hearing is good. He did say moi. I love Prince forever. I wish my neighbours would love him too.

Neighbour

One of my neighbours is very kind. Their family supports "Black Lives Matter" and homosexuality. They are all white people. The parents always play with their children. They are happy. They have two kids, one boy and one girl. I saw that their children have a lot of toys. They are spoiled. Their father is generous and often gives neighbours books for free.

Today the father plays with his children outside. One acquaintance passes by and talks to the father. At the beginning, they are excited and talk about everything. Then the acquaintance feels angry and swears at the father. He said fuck you and you fuck your kids… Finally, he beat the father in front of the children. The acquaintance left. The father calls the police. Police 11 Division officers drive the number 1108 police car came here. They record the father's testimony. They also listen to his kids' words. The two kids are scared and feel angry. They cry. Police officers call the acquaintance and tell him to go to the Police 11 Division to surrender. Then the police officers go.

I saw the whole thing. I learn a lesson. I have bad temper, but I should not fight with people at any time. If the people are angry, I should go away to avoid a confrontation. I was arrested before, because I beat someone. I felt ashamed. I should correct my mistake and remember it forever.

Career at TTC

TTC means the **Toronto** Transit Commission. Every time I take the TTC; I learn a lot. Once I waited for bus number 40 at Kipling subway station. I saw a TTC employee who was crippled but he could still walk fast enough to complete his work. Just after five minutes, I saw another TTC employee who was lame, yet she moved her legs enough speed to clean the station. I know that the TTC pays very good salaries and retirement pensions. The employees work hard and are smart enough to keep their careers at TTC. Their families need money and dignity.

I am not healthy, which sometimes becomes an excuse for me not to find a job. I often think that I should focus on my writing career. Staying at home is not always productive. If I am diligent, I may do much better.

Five years ago, I took the subway to the Young and Bloor intersection. I noticed one TTC employee who cleaned the washrooms. She had downs syndrome. She smiled and kept the washrooms very clean. I was deeply moved. I wish I was a TTC worker and could be useful for others.

TTC drivers do not have easy jobs. If they do not eat enough food, they may develop motion sickness. If they eat more, they may have to go to the washroom often. Also the drivers sometimes drink café or water to keep their minds alert. Yet some long distance buses need to be driven for almost two hours. Now there is the pandemic. The drivers must wear masks. If the drivers wear eyeglasses too, the eyeglasses often get steamed up, which severely impacts the safety of driving.

> *On average, at least one TTC driver gets harassed or threatened every day.*

This is zero tolerance. Passengers and TTC employees should respect each other. The TTC is the best choice for many of us. We hope that our transportations will be faster and cover more areas. These are the TTC current goals as well.

Reference:

On average, at least one **TTC driver gets assaulted** or threatened every day, both Ross and Kinnear told CBC News. Oct. 10, 2015

Discharge

Today, I went to the St. Joseph Hospital Emergency again. There were six police cars from three Police Divisions. I went to the waiting area. Two police officers and one criminal were there. I find that gender sometimes is the first positive appearance. I misjudged one lady police officer; I thought she was a man. She was 1.70 meter tall, her hair was curved and short. I liked her hair. She smiled at me. I originally thought that she was a male police officer, so I felt scared. She was nice to me. The male police officer was bossy. He sat down there and watched everything. The chair was too high for me; I couldn't reach the ground by my feet. I felt so uncomfortable that I sat down on the edge of chair with my feet flat on the ground. The male police officer immediately remind me to up my feet. I up my heel again. The criminal had an observable open wound. She sat in the wheelchair and was sent into the waiting room. Soon, she came out and the nurse said she was discharged. The lady police officer was unpleasant because she knew the woman criminal was quite sick. I saw the male police officer was numbed.

I was the next one. The doctor let me in the waiting room. He touched my wound and found some bottles of medicine for me. I was discharged too.

Stew Eel

For my dear teacher Sean Moore

Today I go to Sun food Supermarket. I buy an over 3 pound eel, which is14 dollars per pound. I spend 42.15 dollars. I also buy winter melon, fresh leafy vegetable, mushrooms, black and white rice.

Since I do not know how to cook eel, the friendly master helps me very much. He did not steal anything and cut eel's most dangerous part off. I feel very satisfied. I come home, find an apron and stew the eel. I first pour a lot of cold water. Then I put the eel like an alive one. I turn on a small fire to stew it. I cut winter melon, twist the leafy vegetable, and put half box of sliced mushrooms. I stew it for 25 minutes then I add rice to it. I find that the rice boiled after 10 minutes. I stop cooking. I taste the soup; it is really delicious.

Do not forget; eat up!

Sun Food Chinese Supermarket

I like Chinatown, mostly because I love Chinese food. Monday, I see my psychiatrist Dr. Desai who has seen me for over five years. He is an Indian gentleman. He asks me many questions. I also wish he could use Freud's methodology to cure my illness. I like and trust him. He is very agreeable.

After visiting, I go to Chinatown Sun Food Supermarket. I see a business man order ten fresh lobsters. They are really good! I feel hungry too and I order the biggest and fattest female lobster. It is very strong and pulls back her big tail fast. It is over 3 pounds and costs me $49.85. The worker chopped the lobster; I saw some dark green liquid come out. The worker put the lobster head in a plastic bag. And the rest is in the other bag. He teaches me how to cook it. He said not to wash it especially the raw lobster brain plasma. Put some oil and steam for 15 minutes with fresh ginger.

I go home. Strictly follow what he said. I can cook the lobster now. The lobster head tastes like egg custard. I love it. The belly of lobster is full of meat. I cannot eat it up for a while. Last time, I cooked lobster congee, I do not know how to eat lobster, so I called my neighbour to teach me. I learnt a lot and this time I can eat it properly by myself. I put the lobster crust in the pot with black and white rice in the big fire with two pieces of well-done pork back bone. Over 50 minutes, the lobster congee is done. I unconsciously, eat the lobster head. The congee's taste exactly like lobster brain plasma. I enjoyed it again. It takes me two days to finish it.

Also, I buy three chops of carp, two big pieces of pork back bone, and some winter melon. I first boil the bone. Then I wash it and the pot that I use to boil the back bone. Furthermore, with water, I put winter melon, onion, ginger, oyster's oil, cooking wine, vinegar, and chicken essence to stew for one hour. That is my favorite food.

I love Chinatown, I like to eat in Chinatown.

Touch Myself

Yesterday, I made a confession to the God Father, who did not punish me. I felt guilty and restless. I watched the discipline video at the church. The nun reminds me to turn down the volume. I tried to let God Father beat me hard so I repented to him. He did not do it and left without warning. I was disappointed and went home. I watched the spanking DVD so additive that I fuck myself. The whole night I could not sleep and beat my butt hard by myself. I must say I am very sorry to Toronto Police 11 Division Inspector Joyce Schertzer, who did not ask me for more silver coins.

Although, this is not my first time I spank myself and fuck myself, yet this is my first time to do so in ten years. I shook my hands fast when I touch my service parts. I even cannot control myself and twist the body in the bed. I want to use self-punishment machine to solve my problems. But I did not have it in my house. I fuck myself bleeding. I never felt so happy and satisfied. The blood is on my bedsheet and my hands. I even felt pain in my waist. I know that I may get an infection. I do not care. I love it and I need it. My butt is red and some places are bruised.

Today, I go to Reconnect (mental illness rehabilitation centre) to change my dressing on my leg. My favorite nurse Jay has a heart-to-heart talk with me. I told him what I did last night. I even took off my pants to show him the marks. I asked him to discipline me now and try his best to make me feel pain. He refused. He suggests that I should see a psychologist who he recommended. I agree. I like him. He always helps us and worries about us and cheers up us. He said that he likes my books and even said that I am brilliant. I told him that, I am so-so and so common. He did not laugh at me at all. He is very knowledgeable and good at psychology and psychiatry. He treats everybody well. I trust him just like I trust my psychiatrist. When I go home, he called me and let me bring the medication to him that I did not take. He will do the needle injection for me on next Monday. I wish that he or my psychiatrist will discipline me hard every day. I hate myself. I want to be good forever.

At 7:30 PM, my friend who takes care of my dog calls me. We talk a lot. I tell him what I did last night and what happened today. He did not console me. On the contrary, he swears at me badly and teaches me a lesson. I know that he is upset with me because I caused so many problems. He said that if I am to continue like that, he will drive two hours to my home to beat me hard and show no mercy. I say sorry to him.

At night, I recall my mistakes. I know that I need to write them down and keep myself awake. I sincerely wish that somebody would cure my shady thoughts.

Thank you Jay and thank you people who care about me and others.

A Pair of Earrings

Reddit is my friend; she is an Italian. She is frank and warm hearted, but sometimes she is rude. I like her partly because she is my late husband's classmate and good friend. Reddit works hard. She always keeps her house clean and tidy. She also likes animals and birds and feeds them regularly. She likes to cling to the powerful. Yet her rich friends never care about her.

I am not rich. I can understand Reddit. I notice that she likes earrings. She has many pairs of earrings, yet seldom real gold. Her mother gave her a pair of Italian pure gold earrings. She rarely wears them. That is why I like her. She has her own mortgage free house and car. She is an upper middle class. I know that she sometimes has parties with her rich friends. I do not want her to look poor. I give her a 10K gold pair of earrings from Hudson Bay Company, which is worth 129 dollars as a New Year gift. When she saw the gift, she is very happy and surprised. She asked me: "You buy them with full price?" I shook my head. She accepted it cheerfully. I felt sensation too. She cherished my gift and does not wear it often. Some of her rich friends laugh at her. Her ear punches are a little bit loose. She wants to be perfect. Reddit knows a jewellery businessman. She goes to his store. She asked how much the pair of earrings are worth. He offers 60 dollars with two price tags of 129 dollars' original box. Reddit refused. She knows that this man can punch ear holes, so she asks for help to punch the pair of earring holes in her ears. Since she is an old customer, he agreed. But he said that as an exchange, she needs to give him the original box. Also, Reddit had better not taken off the gold earrings anymore. She accepted.

The businessman does it very fast and accurate. It is just a little bit of blood.

Reddit feels very satisfied and goes home. The businessman told her do not take a shower within three days. She followed what he said.

Another party comes up. Reddit is invited by her upper-class friends. They just want her to make an exhibition of herself. Yet, Reddit wears her best clothes and wedding ring and her brand new earrings. They notice that her earrings are fixed. She is not shabby at all. She is a popular lady at the party. Yet she is hard to please. She challenges everybody. Finally, they let her go. Reddit does not regret it at all. She gets a successful revenge. That is my friend.

God Father

Near my home, there is a Catholic Church. I love this church because it is open every day. The God Father is a young man, who looks like he is in his 30's. He has a very strong and attractive voice. He is broad-minded. Sometimes I offend him, but he is never angry or blames me. I like him. He speaks English and Spanish very fluently. He likes singing. I often listen to him hum a little song.

Every Thursday is a confession day for the church. I go to the church today. Coincidently, there is a wedding here. The God Father holds the wedding ceremony. The new couple kneel down to listen to his blessing and teaching for almost two hours. He opens the bible and recites the chapters to show God's true essence. He is humorous too. The bride is happy and cheerful. The groom blushes all the time. The wedding finished. We begin the confession.

At the beginning, I think that the severe offenders will be paddled by the God Father, so I take off my underwear and just wear a long skirt. I even whipped myself at home. My butt is still red. I just want him to know that I am a bad one and I deserve to be punished harder. I find that people who make a confession are one by one coming in a small room and sit down to repent to the God Farther. I remembered that people should kneel down to do so. He sits down in the other room. The attached wall between the two rooms has a wood window with a lot of small holes. The God Father listens to the people's confessions and decides how to educate them. The most severe punishment is kneeling down in front of the statue of Mercy Maria holding baby Jesus Christ to confess and pray to be forgiven. I repent: the first time I came to church I did not find the washroom; I could not hold my pee and I also felt embarrassed to bare my butt crouching to do so in public. I stood and took off my underwear to pee behind the statue of the church. Also I use my cellphone watching on-line the spanking DVD in the church. Now I know that the God Father is not like the DVD shown. I put on my underwear and go to the confession room. The God Father greets me first. He is nice to us. I told him what I did in our church. He is not angry and forgives me on the spot. I really feel released. I said that "Father, how old are you?" he joked me and said that: "I am sixty years old." I smiled and asked him whether he wants to marry me or not. He replied me that he already married to the Church; he cannot marry twice in his life. I told him that I am a millionaire. I have my family lawyer and personal accountant. He said that he could not marry me. I am happy that my God Father belongs to our church and me forever.

After confession, we each kneel down to get Holy Communion, I look up him. He said that: "Eat it." I did so. After that he disappeared just like last time. I did not see which door he goes into. I go home too. I really feel that church people are much better than other people. We are pure and kind. Churches are truly God's earthly home.

Terry

Terry is an American citizen, who was a member of our church for decades. He is new to our branch. Two years ago, when he had just joined our branch, he was married here. Bishop Barker performed his wedding. He was a correction officer. He treated jailbirds well. He worked for the CIA for years and then retired. He immigrated to Canada and wanted to live in Toronto for good. He likes people calling him boy, although, he is almost 60 years young. He likes to wear cowboy boots, even for his wedding. Since he was married during COVID-19, he did not have wedding banquet, just a ceremony.

Terry is responsible for opening the church's gate and doors on Sundays. He is not keen to do this job, because he feels it belittles him. I feel in love with him for months. I am always the first person to go into the church on Sundays. He and I see each other alone every time. He often talks to me and we exchange our privacy. Once he showed his new wife's picture from his cellphone. He said that he does not like her, because she often fights with him and broke his skin many places even on his head. I saw the scars too. I gave my books to my church friends; he praised me. I said that: "I am just an amateur writer." He said that: "Your books 'covers are not like those of an amateur." He never boasts what he did in his past. He is modest. I like his personality. I know that he does not love me more than I love him. He is an old fox; I am a chicken. Sometimes, I hate him. He keeps me at arm's length. He is a professional lover. I am really an amateur both in my books and dating.

I cannot wait to see and I did a speech in the church to express my love to him and want to marry him too. He suddenly disappeared from our church. I had no choice and called Bishop Barker for help. At night, Bishop Barker called me. He said that Terry may not like me. He had two children, one boy and one girl from his ex-wife. He was married twice. I am totally lost; he never told me that. I stopped thinking of him. Hopefully, I will find my better half soon.

Neighbours and I

I am an immigrant. I was married to my husband and had a permanent house to live in. I have been very sick because I have mental illness. My beloved husband is 27 years older than me. When we just lived together, I was very shy. I did not speak to my neighbours at all. I felt that they might look down upon me or dislike the Chinese. I had kept that way over half a year. Yet I gradually found that some neighbours greet me often. My husband's best friend whom he called his "big brother" sometimes invited us to his house to chat. He even encouraged me to make friends with his daughter, who was a professor and got a PHD in USA. She is four years older than me and treats me nice. At that time, I already began to write books. They always cheer me up and said that they enjoyed reading my books. Her father wrote book reviews for me. I appreciated his help.

In our marriage, we invited many old neighbours, some of whom live here for generations. They are glad that we are together. We held the wedding in our church and they gave us a lot of wedding gifts.

We have a 135 years old tree in front of our house. In autumn, one neighbour with two young kids helps us clean the leaves. We gave them chocolate for their help. My husband likes children but we do not have any. He often takes care of our neighbour's girls for free. We have three fur ball sons (our three male cats). We pamper them very much.

My husband's classmates from kindergarten to high school still live near us. They go to our home for fun and business. My husband has investments with them. They have cars, so sometimes they drive us to restaurants for dinner. My husband always said that, we enjoy our second childhood.

My husband had cancer. The doctor suggested that he should use cane to walk. My neighbour bought a brand new cane and installed it for him for free. One family helped us cut the lawn for free. When my husband passed away, one neighbour bought a tree from city in memory of my husband. I set up the funeral in our church. I invited our neighbours and friends. Bishop Barker held the ceremony. Some neighbours even went to the graveyard with me. When I came home, I felt very sad. I cried loud. My neighbour went to my home to comfort me.

I have mental illness. Some neighbours do not like me. When I had my puppy, they called the city to fine me and made up stories against me. I had to go to legal aid for help. I even had a rights advisor from the city. Some people throw chocolate into my backyard. I woke up at four am to walk my dog. A neighbour walked her dog and my dog played with her old dog. She screamed and said that my dog bit her old dog. Finally she did not find a wound and let me go. I was very sad and gave away my fur ball baby.

Not all the neighbours are good ones. The only thing I can do is tolerate some of them.

Halloween's Bo

Bo is my tenant Tony's kitten, who is two years old. She wears long pure black fur and has big brown eyes. When I first time saw her, I was surprised and said that "exactly like my cat Prince." She is timid; for almost 20 days she just stays in her owner's room. My cat Prince who has pure black fur coat too, often sits outside the door and watches her. Anyway, Bo is Prince's new girlfriend now.

Time passes quickly. Today is Halloween. Bo comes out of the room and goes to the first floor living room. Prince sleeps in the cat tree and smells her scent. He is very excited and jumps down to the floor. He sniffs Bo; Bo is upset and tries to attack Prince. What is a pussy cat? Since they seldom get together, I take photos for both of them. I love both of them too. Bo just moved here, I cannot let her go to my porch for greeting people. They can show their affection to me on this particular day. Halloween's Bo and Prince brings me double luck! Bo is very light, just a few pounds. Prince is heavy 18 pounds. They are all Bombay Cats, which belong to middle size cat. Bo is wild and aggressive and has a bad temper. She tries to prove that she is the Queen in this house. Prince is mild and gentle. He does not care about Bo's actions and leaves her alone. Bo becomes normal and plays with Prince's toys and sometimes watches me. I give cat treats to them and say "trick or treat!" Bo goes to the treats and walks away. Prince eats up. It is really hard to please Bo. I like to pick up cats. I holds Bo. She panics and scratches me very hard. I let her go. My face is bleeding. It is a bad luck especially in Halloween.

Finally, Bo calms down. I sits down to watch her. She does not like the hustle outside. She ignores Prince too. Prince sleeps in the cat tree again. I said to Bo,

"Do you like to be a bride today?" Bo is purring. I guessed that she said yes. She is the new Queen in my house; my name is Sobchuk lol.

Night is long and endless. I fall to sleep. Bo's owner comes back; I do not know. When I wake up again, I listen to the snoring in their room. How can I mention Bo's engagement to him? I must think it over.

I Am so Lucky

Just like many mental illness patients, I went to the mental illness hospitals many times. Most often the police sent me to the jail and then to the hospitals. In January, 2021 I was very sick and called 911 a lot of times. Unlike the usual, the police 11 Division sent the same two police officers to my home to talk to me and help me. One police officer knew that my knee had problems so he volunteered to walk my German Sheppard Dog. I appreciated this very much. After almost one month, I recovered at home.

Now I study at the Centre Adult Learning Centre instead of staying in the hospital. I feel that I am so lucky. Sometimes, I pass CAMH; I see the familiar faces wandering and even begging on the streets. I knew that we have long way to go for the equality. Now the policy provisions of ODSP are very tough. Disability rate in the world is sky high. We need to find a good way to show our talents. We are gifted. We are not just cleaners or dishwashers … We need more decent careers. The governments should increase the funding for it.

I do not know why some leaders are bad to bone and still there. And why disabled cannot represent ourselves and take a leadership role. We may not be perfect and representable, but some of us are brilliant and deserve good leadership. Campaign is not the only way to choose the MPP and MP. WE NEED A BREAK.

To Our Party

Dear Sir Primer Doug Ford

My name is significant not important. I wish you were still not immersed in the holiday's atmosphere either. The last two times, I emailed you and called you many many times for the suburban and vast countryside poverty. You not only solved it but also made things worse. Justen Trudeau gives a lot of money to some people yet most farmers did not get a penny and are even worse shape. He delivers money to only some during the election campaign. I do not blame him since his father was just like this too.

Please send emergency funds to the countryside and suburbia to correct the situation.

All the best!
24th, Dec 2021

DEAR SIR ARIF VIRANI

THIS IS BIN SOBCHUK. WE ARE FRIENDS FOR A LONG TIME. SINCE WE KNOW EACH OTHER SO WELL, I WANT YOU TO JOIN CONSERVATIVE PARTY CANADA NOW.
AS A MEMBER OF CONSERVATIVE PARTY OF CANADA, I SINCERELY INVITE YOU TO JOIN CONSERVATIVE PARTY TO BEGIN YOUR NEW SUCCESS.

SINCERELY YOURS
BIN SOBCHUK

1106

1106 is a police car which belongs to the Toronto Police 11 Division. I had seen it many times. Every time I see it; I purify myself again.

I know that I am naughty. I always persuade myself by being good and polite. I have bipolar disorder, so my temper sometimes is manic or depressed. I often lose my temper and fight with somebody. Most of the time I am very quiet and funny. Once I had nothing to do and wandered to the LCBO, police car 1106 pass by me and the police officer in the car looks at me. I think that I am wrong for not going to Fresco for food. I like studying; I also like high marks. Once I accomplished a semester; I am very excited and go outside for a walk. I saw 1106 stop on the street and the police officers standing beside the car were friendly. I am glad to see them. I often think about bad things, for example: abusing TTC's fares or not getting off the TTC. 1106 catches me twice, I am admired by them. I randomly see 1106 many times. They are just like my best friends accompanying me for good. I love the Toronto police; I like to be guided by them too

Dear Sir Mayor John

I gave my puppy Buddy to John Poullos who is an animal lover. He ran for the mayor but failed. I love him just like loving a big brother. I call him dear Sir Mayor John. He rents two farms and hires two workers. His partner and her daughter live with him.

They work hard. They have seven horses, forty five cows, five dogs and two cats. John loves these animals and feeds them twice daily no matter whether there heavy rain or snow. Sometimes I call John; he is bone tired. I hope that he is well, because in my mind, he is already my older brother. I often encourage him to run for mayor again. He is hesitant but very ambitious. He has a sense of humor; he likes animals' jokes. Me too. I call him Sir, because I love people who earn money by labour. They are very kind hearted. Once I asked him "Why are you not rich, where is your money?" He smiled and told me "My money is eaten by my animals. None left." He said the truth. His horses and cows shit even can be eaten by animals. They sell the shit which a lot of farmers are eager to buy. Their shit is even higher than the third floor of a house! Yet, when I knew that my puppy Buddy eats the cheapest dog food; my heart is aching. I told him that I buy dog food and mouth wash for your five dogs. Every two months we see each other in my house. That is my happiest time. We chat; I give him some small gifts. He likes them and thanks me. I order food; we eat together. He is poor, every time I see him wearing the same boots. Because of his situation, I made phone calls and emailed Premier Doug Ford and conservative party leader O'Toole to solve the countryside poverty. I do get positive feedback. Thank to my party leaders and people just like us.

Winter in Ontario is harsh especially in the north. They feed animals and clean their shit almost at the same time. Too cold to be delayed. I see John's rough hands, I hope that he is physically well. Recently, I was diagnosed with bone cancer. I do not want to tell him. I am afraid that he will not like me anymore. I often tell myself to be stronger. I have two fur ball sons, Prince (cat) and Buddy (dog). Buddy is a big boy now. He is over two years old and weighs 120 pounds. I love them forever.

Sometimes, I call him Brother John. He may like it since he always smiles. If I do something wrong, I tell him, he teaches me and corrects me. Most often, he will tell me something that he did wrong to make me remember it for good. John can video with the cellphone. He does it a lot. He makes Buddy's videos and sends them to me. I laugh at my Buddy. He also does the other dogs' videos to me. I like them too. Yesterday, John's oldest horse who was 35 years old was put down. He was very sad. I believe that his 35 years old horse can break the Guinness World Records.

Dear Sir Mayor John I hope that no matter what happen to me, please treat Buddy and Prince well. God bless all of you. Amen.

Doctor Smith

My family doctor Smith is a lady. She is the first lady family doctor in my whole life. At the beginning, I did not trust any woman doctors. I always want a second opinion from the opposite sex. Once I went to St. Joseph Hospital Emergency, one gentleman doctor was in charge of me. He delivered the right medicines to me and cured my pain. He saw my medical records and asked me that, "Is Doctor Smith your family doctor." I said yes. He said that her medical records were excellent. He also told me that Doctor Smith was his teacher and taught him how to deliver babies. From now on, I trust her deeply. Doctor Smith always gives us the best referrals.

Once I saw Doctor Smith she warned me that Doctor Wood my knee specialist wanted to do a knee replacement for me. I was scared and doubted Doctor Smith for a long time. I did not contact her for months. I knew that she is four years younger than I. I even tried to change my family doctor! Finally, I refused to do the knee replacement operation.

Today, I passed her office. I do have some concerns so I walk into her clinic. The receptionist informs her of my case. She immediately let me in. I felt so moved. Four days ago, my knees caused severe pain at mid-night. It was heavy snowing, three feet high. I went to St. Joseph Hospital Emergency. The nurse supervised me to take some pills and let me go. I was very surprised. I asked her that "I did not see the doctor yet." She was so rude that she called the hospital security to have me removed. The security twisted both my arms and pushed me to the traffic zone. I told them that in the morning, I would see my specialist Doctor Wood; may I sit in the emergency waiting room? They twisted my arms, grabbed my breasts and push me to the centre of traffic road again. Outside the snow stopped the street cars. I called the TAXI; they said that I need to wait at least two hours. I was so cold and waited outside until 6 am. When I went home, I saw my left arm was bleeding. My gold bracelet was damaged. I cannot lift up my right arm… Doctor Smith called the pharmacist to check my medicines one by one. She was not mad at me to challenge her to refuse to take her meds. She and the pharmacist consulted each other and issued me a new prescription. She did not hold a grudge for me at all.

I remembered that at Christmas, I gave her a silver coin which is worth $395.00. She returned it to me. She is great! She is much younger than I. I love her and I want to be her patient forever.

Prince Edward Island

I like to eat lobsters, partly because my favorite family is from Prince Edward Island. They were my neighbours; we often chat with each other. The most reputable family member is Ms. Oakley. She is over seventy. She has two sons and one daughter. Every year I visit them once or twice. Her oldest son is called John Oakley. He is not the broadcast one. He told me that when he was sixteen years old, his grandfather invited him to PEI, (John was born in Toronto.) He felt he was spoiled. His grandpa went to the sea shore and caught 100 fresh lobsters in one day and put them on the big table. He said to John: "Young guy today you are a millionaire." John ate a lot yet most of the lobsters were rotten or given to their neighbours. John never forgot that when he was sixteen years old, he became a millionaire. He lived in PEI half a year and gained 20 pounds. Now he still mentions that it was the happiest time in his life. Steve Oakley is the second oldest child. He ran a construction company for years. His mom told me that he made the fantastic doors. He had a lot of customers. Yet he had a car accident. His first wife and a daughter died in the accident. He collapsed. Finally, he committed suicide. I missed his funeral. Her daughter is the youngest one. She is beautiful. The whole Oakley family all have blue eyes. She married with a Chinese Canadian and has 3 sons; none have blue eyes. She is divorced and lives with her all sons. I really do not know why she was married at eighteen years old and soon had babies. She is not lazy at all. She works 15 hours per day to support her family. Her sons are clever but all have dark color skin. I like them.

At my wedding, I ordered 4 big lobsters. Secret, I knew that their family loves lobster the most. Ms. Oakley smiled and said to me "Bin, I love your lobsters."

Ms. Oakley is like my mom. Once I was sick and stayed in the hospital. She found some leader and gave me the best room in our unit. She was a register nurse, and also a teacher for training nurses. She teaches me and serves me food; of course, I bring gifts for them every time. They also give me gifts. Ms. Oakley is a widow, she never tells me anything about it. She just said that her husband died from colon cancer. I had no relatives in Canada, so every year I go to her home for Christmas or New Years. Now it is a pandemic, they can say no to me.

John is my best friend. Seven years ago, they invited my late husband and me to their home for dinner in Christmas. That was the last time they saw my late husband alive. I recalled that they and my late husband were so funny and talked loudly to each other. I was a dummy. John boasted that one day he will go back to PEI, and shovel us there. We were very excited.

Staying together is my happiest time. I could not forget. I hope that we could keep our friendship forever.

Purgatory

Margret is a single and over 40's. She does not think that she is very attractive. She loves her mentor who is also her friend. He gives her advice and all kinds of help. Recently, she is restless; she needs to be satisfied. Margret goes to her mentor's home and he talks some business about their stocks and taxes. She does not have any interest. She is a lucky girl. She often makes the right decision. Sometimes she is wrong; her mentor will correct it immediately.

Today she is bold and impatient. She talks about making love… her mentor stands beside her and makes coffee. She cannot control herself and pulls off his pants. She astonished, because he did not wear his underwear. She did oral sex with him. He felt that everything is too strange, but let it go. She did a long time blow job; he had no patience. He said naughty girl. She asked him why he did not wear any underwear. He said that he did it since he was a university student. The professors punished the students' bare butts so they did not wear under wear. Second time Margret brings a paddle. She told him that if she does something bad, he can punish her at any time. She is serious. She lusts of sexual desire, yet she knows it is wrong. He did use the paddle to punish her many times and refused sex with her too. Every time, she takes off the underwear, and puts on the arms of the seat. Her butt is high up and he brandishes the paddle for corporal punishment. She feels good and released. The new problem comes out. The mentor feels that his arms are not comfortable; he is over 70th. He did not punish her with the paddle again… She is sad now and has no other choice. She is lonely and an immigrant. One day, she begins her blow job again. He is tolerant. She admires him for a long time. He always said that you can find someone younger. Now he still does not want to marry her. They are a secret couple. They love each other and help each other. Margret read the book and learned how to "smoke". It is useful, at least he said so. Every time she feels high, she wants his severe punishment. He does not do so. She is so confused that she often slaps herself in front of him. At night, she is empty. She watches TV, calls friends, and plays with the cats. She is afraid of the quiet.

She recalled that her mentor did hand jobs for her. He puts three fingers in her vaginal and goes circle. She feels in heaven. But she does not know that it is right or wrong, since her bishops always teaches her there should be no adultery. She begs him to slap her face or breast to stop her lust. He does not do it. He said that no punishment is also a punishment to her. He is old yet still strong. He ejaculates many times in one week. Margret swallows it or let it go. She wishes that he could say yes, when he feels satisfied. He seldom gives her this positive feedback. He also said that his penis is sore. This time, he is pretty angry. He curses that she wastes his time; he has many things to do every day. She feels extremely sorry and guilty. In his whole life, he just had one girlfriend, when he was twenty one years old at his university. He never married and had no children. He studies every day. He said that coffee is his oil to get him moving. She wants him to spank her now. He refused. She puts his belt on her butt. He does nothing. She repents and will not come the whole week. She is afraid of her mentor since he is her idol and economic pole. Although she is a millionaire, she always thinks that she does not match him. He is a so tall, knowledgeable, and multimillionaire. Yet sometimes, he is also a fall guy. When he occasionally loses money in the stocks, she will joke with him a lot. He also blames her as a pop drinker and "Garfield". She does not care at all about this. She is used to it.

He did not marry her mainly because that his brother did not want the property lost. He said that they are eight people (his brother and wife and three nieces and their husbands) He just one person. Margret understood him well. He works very diligently, which wins the heart of Margret. In her mind, he is the smartest. She looks forward to a regular couple's life. She cannot find it. She has no kids, so she is cozy.

At midnight, the hell's fire burns and so that Margret cannot sleep. She sincerely hopes that she can find a final result for it.

Body Camera

Margret has arthritis and her right knee has a sharp pain. She felt helpless. Finally, she went to the hospital emergency by taxi. She was hungry because the whole day she did not eat anything. She could not move so she did not cook either. There are five police cars from three Police Divisions outside the emergency entrance. Margret found a corner to sit down. A young woman in her twenties sat down in the middle row. She was well dressed and restless. Two male police officers and a criminal walked toward her. Margret noticed that one police officer turned on his body camera and watched that woman. The woman also noticed it. She found her cellphone and took off her shawl. She took a picture of that police officer. Her skin is shinny. She is very pretty. That police officer was very embarrassed. He lowered his head and turned off his body camera.

The criminal is a girl too. Her head was broken and bandaged with medical gauze. Her face had blood on it too. She sat down there and yelled. She complained that she did not get fair treatment. She was thirsty, yet the police officers drank coffee. She cried a lot. Margret felt sympathy for that girl. She gave her a can of Pepsi.

Margret was lame. The police staff sergeant noticed it. His uniform is beautiful with one white crown and three white arrows on each shoulder. He watched Margret. He found that she shook her right leg up and down slowly. He took off his mask and police body camera. He sat down facing Margret. Four eyes saw each other. He opened his legs slowly. Margret was surprised. She saw that the two police officers from the other side watched it too. She did not know that she did the right thing or not. Of all the police officers in the emergency, the staff sergeant has the highest rank. Margret thought that she should give him the pop and let him give it to that girl. At least, she did not think that he wanted to make a girlfriend of the 270 pounds girl. Another criminal is a man. He had a Hiccup. The two police officers who monitored him laughed at him.

It was Margret's turn. She went to the room to wait for the doctor. She still thought about the meaning of what the staff sergeant did. He reminded her not to make friends with the criminals.

Printed in the United States
by Baker & Taylor Publisher Services